TRACY: MAIL ORDER BRIDE

THE CHRISTMAS BRIDES OF JEFFERSON CITY
BOOK 7

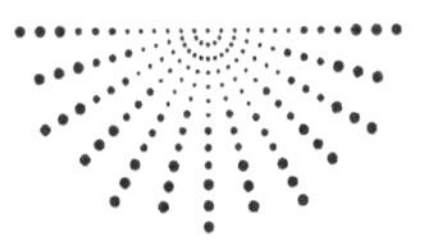

INDIANA WAKE

BELLE FIFFER

The Christmas Brides of Jefferson City

Everything was in bloom in Jefferson City at the beginning of summer but the Mayor had only one thing on his mind. He wanted to find wives for his sons by Christmas!

Mayor Arnold Foster is a dominant man that not many want to cross. When he demands that Pastor Thomas Brooks find Mail Order Brides for all *Six* of his sons the good pastor is reluctant. The Mayor will not be thwarted and resorts to threats. Pastor Brooks reluctantly agrees, knowing that he is the better person to take care of the women than whomever the mayor would get next.

Mayor Foster's sons are in no hurry to marry, in fact, they are totally against anything their father could suggest. Six strong and stubborn men will not be easy to persuade.

Pastor Brooks must rely on his faith and strength of character to find the perfect women for the Foster men. He is determined to find matches that will bring love and peace into all the lives of those involved.

Will Pastor Brooks succeed in bringing love to Jefferson City just in time for Christmas?

The books in this series each tell a complete story of one couple

The Christmas Brides of Jefferson City

Nicola

Amy

Polly

Shelley

Anne

Jacira

Tracy

CHAPTER ONE

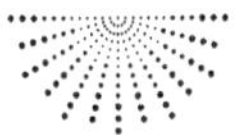

Tracy finished the final stitch. Her fingers were sore from all the sewing, but it was worth it. The hem was finally finished. It had been so easy to do as the dress wasn't moving around anywhere. Sewing it on a dummy and not on her sister was certainly the better alternative. Why didn't she do that to start with? A smile crossed her face; if they had, they wouldn't have spent an hour bickering and her stitches going everywhere.

But the wedding dress was done now, and all that was needed was for Polly to try it on to check for any finishing touches. Tracy put aside her needle and thread and rose to her feet.

"There." She bit back a wince as her legs

straightened out. She had spent too much time crouching on the floor. "That's done."

Polly looked up from her book. She had been relegated to the bed when Tracy finally put her foot down, and she had quietened her sulking after a book had been practically shoved into her face. Now her eyes widened and she stared at the dress hanging on the dummy Tracy had snagged from their landlady's room.

"Oh my, Tracy!" she gasped. She threw her book aside and got to her feet. "That is just stunning."

Tracy laughed.

"You were here watching me all the time I was putting it together!"

"I stopped paying attention after a while. You know what I'm like." Polly ran a hand over the sleeve of the dress. "It's beautiful."

"Thank you." Tracy was still smiling as she started to put things into her sewing basket. She did know her sister and she had little patience. "Mother was a good teacher when it came to sewing our own things."

Polly wrinkled her nose.

"Good teacher? I was terrible at it."

"Only because you weren't able to sit still long enough to pay attention." Tracy shook her head. "How you managed to listen long enough to Father when he taught you how to use a rifle, I have no idea."

"Because I like shooting things." Polly shrugged. "I didn't like stabbing myself in the hand with a needle."

Polly was one of those people that needed to keep on the move. She could not sit still. It was a wonder she didn't fall out of bed with the amount of tossing and turning she did when they had shared a room. But somehow, Polly was able to be still and silent when going hunting. Tracy had never figured out why Polly couldn't harness that skill for things that were actually needed, although somehow Polly knew how to cook. It was a wonder the workers at the ranch hadn't been poisoned yet.

Morgan was going to have his work cut out for him. He was going to marry a woman who knew how to cook and hunt and could vaguely clean, but she wouldn't be able to sew his shirts back together or add any fine details to things. Thankfully, the two of them weren't materialistic and preferred simple things. And Morgan knew how to sew, which had surprised Tracy. Where they grew up, men just didn't do that. Out West, things had a slight shift. Men had needed to learn how to take care of themselves as well, and the Foster brothers were very self-sufficient.

Tracy picked up her sewing basket and placed it on the bed.

"You're going to look beautiful at your wedding, Polly. Morgan's jaw is going to drop when he sees you."

"I hope so. It takes a lot to surprise Morgan, and I want to be able to do that." Polly turned to her sister. "I want to thank you, with the help you've been giving us with our dresses over the last weeks, I think all the Foster brothers jaws are going to be dropping."

Tracy felt a warmth swelling in her stomach. She had been honored that all the girls, even Jacira, had come to her and asked her to help with their wedding dresses. There was a professional seamstress in town, but it was too much for her to do at such short notice, so Tracy had offered to help out. She loved to sew, and there wasn't much to do as Thomas's housekeeper once she had cleaned his house top to bottom. He was a simple man and barely made a mess. Tidying up after a tidy man was easy.

At least it was simple work, and Tracy did get to be in his presence. That was a plus for her, even if it did mean staring at him wishing she was brave enough to say something. Polly had talked about being around someone you loved and being unable to say anything about it due to nerves was hard. Tracy found it excruciating.

If only I were one of the brides tomorrow. That would make me the happiest woman alive. Aside from Polly and my friends, that is.

"I still wonder how the day is going to go when we've got six weddings to get through and then a Christmas reception afterward." Polly flopped back onto the bed, almost sending Tracy's sewing basket flying. "Surely, that shouldn't be possible."

Tracy sighed and picked up the things that had bounced out, closing the lid.

"I'm sure it will have been figured out by now. You'll probably get married at the same time and the vows go down the line. Or they do it in order, which means you'll be first, seeing as Morgan's the eldest son."

"Great." Polly groaned. "I just have to be first, don't I?"

"You'll be fine, honey. It's going to be a great day."

For the most part. Tracy was happy for her sister, for her friends. They were marrying good men who had been very stubborn but had softened over the last year. Having a father they hated ship in women to be their brides had certainly brought out their stubborn side. Tracy laughed as she remembered their faces. Square jaws clamped tight, steely eyes refusing to look at the beautiful women before them. In the end, they had learned that the women had nothing to do with their father and that Pastor Thomas, who had chosen them, had done well.

Tracy had guessed they would give in eventually and stop being so hard-headed, but there had been times when she wondered if she had pushed a little too much and it wasn't going to happen. Thomas had thought the same, and Tracy had been the one to push her insecurities aside and tell him that it was going to be fine.

She knew, in her case, it wasn't stubbornness. It was nerves. Fear of losing more than just Thomas's affection.

"How was it possible that only a year ago we were receiving letters from Jefferson City at Christmas looking for husbands, and less than three-hundred-and-sixty-five days later all of us are getting married?" Polly asked.

"Things can change in a year..." Tracy paused. "What do you mean, all of us?"

Polly's expression softened. She took Tracy's hand.

"You could be part of it as well. If you just tell him the truth."

Tracy decided for a moment to play dumb, but she couldn't do that to Polly. Her sister was far too astute. A lump formed in her throat and Tracy forced herself not to cry. She had been doing a lot of that lately, and she didn't want to do it anymore.

"I... I can't." She sagged onto the bed beside her sister. "I just can't."

"You seriously can't tell the man you love that you want to be with him?" Polly snorted. "It's been clear to us that you fell in love when you were exchanging all those letters. And I'm not surprised: he's handsome and sweet in a nice tidy package."

"Polly!"

"And I can tell that he's mad about you, too. Why don't you say something?"

Tracy knew the reason why. It had been playing on her mind since she arrived, and it was something she hadn't been able to divulge to anyone. Not even her sister. If she had, Polly would certainly have gone to Thomas and told him to buck his ideas up. Tracy didn't want that.

She stared at her hands in her lap.

"I haven't said anything because I know there's going to be rejection. And trouble."

"Trouble?"

"I wasn't brought here for Thomas Brooks."

Polly rolled her eyes.

"Who cares if you weren't? We can't help who we fall in love with, and it's not fair for you two to suffer in silence because you believe you shouldn't marry a man you didn't come here for."

"That's not my thoughts of the matter, Polly. I know that's going to be Thomas's reasoning when I tell him my feelings. I don't want to have that hurt me." Tracy swallowed. It was already hurting her, knowing it was there. "There's another reason as well. The main one why I can't tell Thomas the truth. You know what I'm talking about."

Polly did. "You mean Mayor Foster, don't you?"

Tracy nodded. "He's threatened to take Thomas's job away, to ruin him, if he doesn't do as Foster wants."

"But Thomas has matched all of the Foster sons now. He's got nothing to worry about regarding his job. It was all as Foster wanted."

"Except me," Tracy said bitterly. She felt a knot forming in her stomach. "Mayor Foster has his eye on me. And I know he wants to have me as his wife."

The thought really did turn Tracy's stomach. She didn't care for Arnold Foster at all. He was a slippery character, and he always put her on edge. He reminded her of their creepy neighbor back home, the one who would find reasons to come over and just leer at her. Tracy had been glad to get away from him, but she hadn't wanted her weird neighbor to follow them in another form. Foster would find excuses to be around her over the last six months. Tracy worked as a housekeeper for Thomas but also did a few cleaning jobs for other townspeople who weren't able to afford a live-in servant. She didn't mind; it kept her busy and she was building a nice reputation for herself. But Foster seemed to know where she was and would make sure to be passing by whenever she was working or be in the morning room of her clients as a guest. And he would just stare at her. Tracy hadn't been this uncomfortable in a long time, and she tried to keep her distance.

She had thought about telling Thomas about it, that she was concerned about Foster's intentions. But what could Thomas do? He couldn't ask him not to follow her around, not when he had no say in Tracy's life. There wasn't much he could do, and Tracy didn't want to put Thomas in the firing line. It wasn't fair on him.

It's not fair on you and you're the one who's having to deal with a creepy mayor.

"But... you..." Polly's face slackened as her mouth dropped open. "You'd be Morgan's stepmother as well as his sister-in-law. Isn't that just the oddest thing?"

"I don't think Foster would care if it does look odd. He knows what he wants, and that's me." Tracy's hands clenched into fists. "I know he wants to see me at his house. Tonight. Thomas said that he wants to spend Christmas Eve with a few close friends. A dinner party of some sort and exchange gifts at midnight. Somehow I know it's going to be a dinner party for two and that a wedding ring is involved."

"You really think he's going to propose?"

Tracy snorted.

"I'm not stupid, Polly. I know what he's up to. For months he's been cornering me, and recently he's trying to allow me to have him visit as a suitor. I've always told him no and to go away, but he keeps pestering me." Tracy found herself standing and pacing the room. Her agitation was beginning to build. "He's telling Thomas to make sure that I'm there. I already know that I don't want to go anywhere near him. But if I don't, Thomas gets targeted."

That was what made Tracy really angry. Foster had been threatening Thomas's job and reputation for a year now. If Thomas didn't get the girls, Foster would take his job away. If Thomas didn't have the Foster brothers married by Christmas, Foster would take his job away. If Tracy didn't go to Foster's house when he wanted, Foster would make sure Thomas was run out of town. If it wasn't his way, then he would make sure whoever stopped it from happening suffered. Tracy wasn't about to let Thomas go through that.

But she wasn't about to be a lamb to the slaughter and go to him. It might have been just the two of them and Tracy would be able to walk out, but if it was an actual party and there were people as witnesses, Tracy knew it would be more embarrassing. She didn't want to put herself through it, especially with a man she intensely disliked.

"He can't target Thomas!" Polly scowled. "That's ridiculous! Thomas is a good man, and his services are always packed. Everyone loves him."

"I know that, but you know how quickly a smear campaign can manifest. I don't want that for Thomas." Tracy rubbed her hands over her face. She felt sick. "And I know it'll be worse if Foster knows that I'm in love with Thomas. He'll see it as a betrayal and still blame Thomas for that."

It wasn't fair. Tracy had hoped for a new life elsewhere, and she had gotten that - Tracy loved Jefferson City - but she had ended up falling for a man who would end up being run out of town because she didn't fall in love with a particular person. It was almost like dealing with a child. A child who was far too influential.

Tracy wished she could just leave. Maybe she could leave with Thomas. Or she could leave and persuade Thomas to stay. One thing she knew for sure, she was not going to marry Arnold Foster. Not a chance.

"Oh, Tracy." Polly's expression softened. She rose to her feet and clasped Tracy's hands. "This is a mess for you. And I thought I was mad for falling for a gruff lawman."

"Morgan's a good man deep down. You saw that for yourself."

"And Thomas is the same. He will stand up for you when push comes to shove."

Tracy sighed. "I don't know about that. Thomas doesn't like to rock the boat. He's barely raised his voice."

That was what Tracy loved about him. He was such a laid-back, placid person. If he knew there was something to fight for, Tracy knew he would step up, but he needed to know it was there first.

"Then you're going to have to do the rocking."

"What?" Tracy blinked. "Stand up to Foster?"

"You're the one he's pestering, isn't he? You tell him to back off. Give him a few home truths." Polly squeezed her hands. "Then Thomas will realize that fighting his feelings for you isn't worth unhappiness for both of you."

Tracy could only hope that her sister was right.

"Thank you so much for doing this with me, Michael." Thomas smiled at the older man across the table. "I'm definitely going to be needing some help with this."

Michael laughed.

"Considering you're marrying six couples in one morning, I'm not surprised you need help." He picked up his glass and took a sip. "I'm just surprised you agreed to this."

So was Thomas. Initially, there had been talk about having one wedding a day, but then the brothers got together and decided to make Christmas by everyone getting married together. Thomas had been silently wishing that they would stick with their original plan of a marriage each day, mostly to stick it to Mayor Foster. The Mayor wanted one big wedding and Thomas wanted to be able to take something away from his wants and needs. He knew it was rather petty by that point, but Mayor Foster had it coming.

At least he would have backup. Michael Davis had come over from the next town to help out - six weddings was a lot in one day, especially when they were all at the same time. With Michael's help, Thomas wasn't going to be floundering. And there would be someone to steer Foster away if he started something. Michael was a big, solid man. A man of God but one who knew when he had to stand his ground. Coming from a different town, Mayor Foster had no hold on him and Michael had no qualms about going toe-to-toe with the mayor.

Thomas cut into his chicken. They were at the restaurant down the street from the church for their lunch, Thomas's inability to cook being the driving force. That is, he could cook but not very well, and he didn't really want his friend to have an upset stomach on Christmas Day. It was a lot easier for someone else to feed him. Tracy would have done it, but she was doing some finishing touches to Polly's dress.

Tracy. The mere thought of her had Thomas's chest tightening. He was such a coward when it came to her.

"How're things going to go, then?" Michael asked as he speared a vegetable with his fork. "Do you know yet?"

Thomas shrugged.

"I'm split between doing it as a big exchange of vows or starting from the oldest Foster and work my way down the line. Although, I don't think Sheriff Chris would be too impressed at being left at the end." Thomas chuckled.

"If that's how it's going to work, then tough to him. You do what you're comfortable with." Michael nodded. "Don't focus on anything but getting them married. This is going to be a very big day already, being Christmas."

"I know." Thomas made a face. "Mayor Foster's going to be really pleased about it. He's been strutting around like Mrs. Casey's cockatoo when it's been preening and wants to show off."

The comparison had been made to him by Mrs. Casey herself, and Thomas had almost choked when he heard it. It was the best way to describe Arnold Foster, who had grandiose ideas far above his station. He was a small, squat guy with a lot of ideas that catered to what he wanted instead of what everyone else wanted. Thomas often wondered what he was trying to prove; it was like Foster was trying too hard and it came across in the wrong way.

It was certainly coming out in a bad way right now.

"Interesting description, but very apt. It's what he normally does." Michael glanced up. "Although that's not what you're worried about, is it? Is something wrong with Miss Brown?"

Thomas almost choked on his chicken. Coughing, he grabbed his water and gulped it down. Even then, he was still gasping for air, hitting his chest with his fist. He stared at Michael, who was giving him a knowing look.

"What... how did...?"

"I've seen the way you are around her whenever I've visited. It's clear you're in love with her, and that you're too scared to tell her." Michael sighed. "Dear Thomas, your confidence always stopped you from getting what you really wanted."

Thomas was still reeling. He had never confessed to anyone that he was in love with Tracy. That was a secret he kept to himself. If Michael Davis, the man who was so wrapped up in spreading God's word, had noticed, then the chances were that everyone else knew about it.

"I didn't think you'd actually notice anything," he said lamely.

Michael rolled his eyes.

"Honestly, Thomas, you think I'm a doddery old man who wouldn't notice a hand in front of my face."

"That wasn't my..."

"I may have promised devotion to God for pretty much all my life, but I'm not blind. You're mad about her, aren't you?"

Thomas decided against denying it. Michael was,

after all, his confessor, even though Thomas hadn't used him as a confessor in a while. He glanced around them, hoping that the busy restaurant wouldn't hear them; he didn't want this spread about if it was still relatively unknown.

"I am." He rubbed his chest, but it didn't ease the pain. "And Mayor Foster thinks she's going to be his new wife. He's dead set on it."

"I see." Michael nodded slowly. "And what does Miss Brown think about it? Does she know?"

"Oh, I'm sure she knows. She's a smart woman. And she doesn't like him at all. The last time Foster came to the house and Tracy was present, Tracy ended up crying because she didn't want to be near him... he made her very uncomfortable."

It had hurt Thomas to see her like that. She was a strong woman, but some things were hard to cope with for all of us, this must be awful for her to think about. It also made him feel as if he had let her down. When the mayor had insisted he bring the women here one of the reasons he gave in was to make sure that they were looked after. He gave his word to God that he would see them in good marriages, marriages they wanted or he would see them cared for until those marriages happened. Could he really let the mayor take Tracy as his wife?

"I see." Michael drawled. "Makes you want to be the big man and hold her tight, and never let go."

Thomas growled.

"You're a word I wish I could use right now, Michael, do you know that?"

Michael grinned.

"I might be thirty years your senior, but I know how to hold myself in a fight. Especially when it comes to words. Why do you think I'm so successful in filling my church every week?"

"Maybe because the ladies think a silver-haired man is attractive?" Thomas shot back. "And you give them a lot of attention."

He had been a little envious about that. Thomas didn't know his full parentage as he had been raised an orphan. His skin was darker than most and he tanned so darkly that some believed he had slave blood in his veins, maybe he did but God didn't judge. At first, there had been a bit of resistance from

Jefferson City about having him as a pastor. But with Michael's help and influence, people had given him a chance. Now they accepted him as one of their own. They loved his sermons and he knew that he was good for the town but meeting people one to one or in smaller groups was still a little awkward for him.

Thomas had never had the same charm as a man like Michael. There was some doubt in his mind, over what he didn't know. It was some lack of confidence that went away in front of his congregation but in smaller groups... it came back. There were times when Thomas wished he could just walk into a room and people wouldn't need time to warm up to him, that they would flock to him immediately without any concerns. Michael could do that easily, and he knew how to turn on the charm. Thomas felt like he was being false if he tried to charm people where Michael did it with ease and comfort.

"There's nothing wrong with looking pleasant for the ladies." Michael smoothed a hand over his hair. "They're the people who bring the men in. You don't need to use God's word to bring the men to church. You get their wives to do it. They're the driving force behind everything."

"For someone who's been declared a lifetime bachelor, you do have a strange way of regarding women."

"It's a necessity and God understands." Michael grinned and winked at him.

Thomas grunted. He started to cut into his potatoes. His stomach was flip-flopping between hunger and nausea, but he wasn't about to pass up on his meal. Not when the owner and his wife were constantly going between tables and would chastise him for not eating. They meant well, and their food was delicious, but Thomas wasn't about to explain himself to them. It would be around town by Christmas morning, and he didn't want that.

It was nobody's business, and yet here he was discussing it with his friend and mentor. Thomas could only hope nobody was close enough to hear them.

"Well, Foster doesn't understand women at all." Thomas chewed his food and swallowed. "Or that Tracy wants nothing to do with him. He thinks he can be charming, but it's like having a snake come after you with that smile. And... he wants her at his place tonight for dinner. Said it was a dinner party, but I have a feeling he's either going to have it as just the two of them or he will propose to her in front of people so Tracy can't be impolite."

Thomas sincerely hoped it was the former, although he didn't like the thought of Tracy being in the presence of that man without a witness. She would be too nice to refuse if it was in front of guests, especially those who would make her feel even worse.

"What does Miss Brown say about it?" Michael asked.

"She immediately said there was no way she was going near him. She has no intention of going unless she's dragged there kicking and screaming."

That had made Thomas a little smug. Foster had to know he was fighting a losing battle. Tracy may not be able to get out of a Society embarrassment, but she could certainly try not to get there in the first place.

"Sounds like Foster isn't going to give up, though," Michael mused.

"When he's got a demand or a want, he goes after it. It doesn't matter what it is, or what other people think, it will be his eventually... and that includes Tracy."

"And it kills you."

It wasn't a question. Thomas put his cutlery down and rubbed his hands over his face. He wasn't just feeling sick, he was suffering from a bad headache. No matter what Tracy said, Foster would make it his way. She was stuck, no matter what. And Thomas hated that.

"What do I do? Foster will be coming to me demanding that I drag Tracy over to his house if she's not there on time. I won't do it, I won't force anyone into something they don't want to do... but if I don't he will just get someone else to do it for him. Maybe he will threaten her sister or her friends? The man is a snake and one way or another he always gets his own way." Thomas felt a wave of anger inside him that he had not experienced in years. The thought of Tracy being harmed or forced to bow to Arnold Foster's will was unbearable. If he wasn't a man of God he would go over there and teach the mayor a lesson... what could he do to keep her safe?

"Maybe if Miss Brown is distracted doing something else and tied up with other activities, that should stop him from getting her." Michael looked pensive. "From what I hear, James Foster is having an early Christmas dinner with his brothers and their brides this evening. He invited us via me to join them, and I know Miss Brown is going to be there. That is going to be a perfect excuse not to be with Mayor Foster, we just have to make sure she stays there."

Thomas thought about it. Foster wasn't really on speaking terms with his sons, and they preferred to treat him as an annoying relative who lives close by but they don't have much to do with him. Nobody would want their controlling father at the Christmas dinner, and if anything did happen, Tracy had six men standing behind her ready to throw Foster out of there. Not to mention Polly would probably get a shotgun and brandish it in Foster's face. That wouldn't be a surprise to Thomas if she did that.

That sounded like the best thing for Tracy right now. She had wedding duties to focus on, and she was supporting her friends and her sister. None of that would matter to Foster, but as long as Tracy was whisked away quickly enough and kept in among her group of friends, Foster wouldn't be able to get to her.

It sounded ridiculous - they were grown-ups, after all - but having Tracy somewhere that Foster wouldn't venture to on his own was the best option. Thomas didn't think having Tracy at his house for dinner or her alone in the boarding house was a good idea.

Dinner at your home would be fine if you were able to stand up to Foster. But you can't. You coward.

Shut up!

"It's just an option to make sure Miss Brown's safe. Keep her as busy as possible. Also," Michael added with a meaningful look and a slight twitch of his mouth, "you need to find time to talk to her. About you two."

Thomas groaned.

"You know I don't know if I can do that, Michael."

"You need to get over your lack of confidence when it comes to women, Thomas. Especially Tracy Brown." Michael picked up his glass of water and looked at Thomas over the rim as he took a sip. "If you don't want to lose her because you're too scared to say anything, someone else is going to come along and you'll miss your chance. You don't want that, do you?"

Thomas glared at his friend. He hated that he was right about this. It just made him feel worse.

CHAPTER THREE

"Come on, Tracy." Polly stood in the doorway of Tracy's room. "Let's go. Morgan's here."

Tracy sat on her bed and stared at herself in the mirror. She had picked out her best dress, and her hair was done up, but she couldn't bring herself to admire how good she looked. She was a bundle of nerves, knowing that even as she was trying to enjoy herself with people she liked, Foster was going to come looking for her when he realized she wasn't coming.

"I..." She licked her lips and clamped her hands between her knees to stop them from shaking. "I'm not sure if I can."

Polly sighed and entered the room, she knelt before her sister and took her hands.

"Come on. We're all celebrating at James's ranch because it's the only place that can house all of us for dinner without the place bursting at the seams. Amy's cooking is something to die for, and I'm so hungry that might just happen... but I can't leave without you."

"I can't." Tracy swallowed. "I know something's going to go wrong."

"Nothing's going to go wrong. It's all taken care of." Polly frowned. "You're scared someone's going to find you and make a scene about you going to Foster's, aren't you?"

"You know I am. I know he's going to try once he finds out that I'm not coming to his house."

"You've told him many times that you want nothing to do with him. A decent man would stop when he knows he's not going to get anywhere."

"But Mayor Foster isn't a decent man," Tracy pointed out. "I don't think he's got a decent bone in his body. He does nothing that benefits anyone else, that is."

"Fair point." Polly squeezed her hands and gave Tracy a gentle smile. "Look, big sister, you're not going to cause trouble at all for anyone."

"I never said anything about that."

"You didn't need to. I know you. Also, the sooner we get to the ranch, the sooner we can keep you and Foster apart. Foster isn't going to go wading into the midst of his sons who dislike him to get you... and if he does we are all there to keep you safe."

Tracy snorted. Foster could certainly try it, and he would definitely cause a scene. As long as he got what he wanted he didn't care. Tracy had never met anyone so spoiled, and they had lived in a fairly affluent part of their hometown where spoiled brats were rife among the adults, never mind the children.

"Tracy, you need to stop thinking." Polly tapped the side of Tracy's head. "I can hear things turning in there. Foster can try to take you away, but he won't get to do it. His sons won't allow that to happen. They're not afraid to stand up to him." She rose to her feet and tugged at Tracy's hands. "Now, come on. Please? I want you to be there, Tracy. Please?"

Tracy allowed her little sister to pull her upright. She couldn't really fight back when it was Polly. She still had misgivings, and Tracy was nervous about bringing this to James's front door; he didn't need his father causing mayhem at Christmas. But Polly wanted her there, and last Christmas Tracy had spent rather miserable because it wasn't the big happy family she wanted. That had been lost a while ago. This time, there was a family, and they had included her. Tracy wanted to be with her friends, those who loved her.

Even though she knew what she wanted, that fear at the back of her mind was still niggling away. Foster was going to find a way to ruin it.

Just as long as I get to see Thomas. That will make my Christmas if I'm able to see him, even though it will be just for a short while.

Maybe the New Year would be a fresh start for her. Maybe she should consider heading elsewhere and starting afresh. Maybe she could get away from Foster and his leering. If she was lucky, she could get

Thomas to come with her. Foster would be trying to run him out of town, so he would be looking for a place to go. Tracy could ask him to come along and they could start out alone.

You have to get past your nerves and actually tell him how you feel, you fool. He's not going anywhere with you unless you actually say something to him!

Grabbing her shawl, Tracy hurried after Polly, who was still holding onto her hand. She nearly stumbled but managed to catch her footing before they reached the stairs. Polly was very eager to get out of there, which Tracy could understand. They had an escort, and he was waiting for them. Polly was testy when she was keeping people waiting.

Morgan was outside with the wagon, keeping the horses from getting too agitated. One horse was starting to stamp its feet eager to be on the move. He hurried over as Polly and Tracy came out and gave them a relieved smile.

"Thank goodness for that." He gave Polly a quick kiss. "I was beginning to think you were never coming out."

Polly rolled her eyes with a smile.

"You could have come up to get us."

"And have your landlady scold me for being anywhere near your bedrooms? I'm not going through that again."

Polly giggled and kissed his cheek.

"Well, that's for waiting."

Morgan grunted, but he gave Polly the sweetest look that Tracy felt the tears well up – would she ever have such love? Morgan was a gruff man with a stubborn streak, but he was a soft, sweet man underneath. Just what Polly needed. She would love to have a man look at her like that.

"Well, your carriage awaits." Morgan took Polly's hand and led them to the wagon. "I'm sorry it's open-top in this weather, but James doesn't know what a closed wagon is. I swear he's the only person I know who can walk around in the snow with just a vest and jeans on and not get frostbite."

"James is an interesting individual." Polly glanced back at Tracy, her eyes glinting. Tracy laughed and held up her hands.

"No comment. I'm not falling for that one, Polly."

Morgan laughed.

"Can't be any worse than what we've called him over the years." He held out his hand and helped Polly up to the seat. Then Morgan turned to Tracy, who was wrapping the shawl about her shoulders. He gave her a gentle smile and took her hand. "Don't you worry about anything, Tracy, we'll look after you."

"How did...?"

Tracy sighed. Of course, he would know. Polly would tell Morgan everything. In just a short space of time, Polly had begun to value Morgan as someone she could talk to about anything. Tracy didn't know how good a sounding board Morgan was, but if it worked for Polly, all good for her. Just not when it came to her own problems.

Then again, there was a good chance most of Jefferson City knew about the mayor's fancy for her. They would be wondering when the wedding bells were going to happen. Tracy fought down a shudder.

"I feel like a weak person with everyone looking after me," Tracy grumbled. "I can take care of myself."

"We never doubted that, and don't be daft." Morgan

urged her up to the seat and walked around the wagon. "You looked after us, and now we can look after you. It's only fair."

Tracy was left stumped at that reply. She honestly didn't know how to respond to that. Morgan climbed up into the seat next to Polly and got the horses in motion. Tracy jerked back as the carriage moved forward, and the horses picked up to a brisk trot almost immediately. Polly tugged her shawl tighter around her shoulders and shivered.

"I should have put on a coat instead of a shawl," Polly grumbled. "It's colder than I expected."

"You're the one who wanted to look beautiful," Tracy pointed out. "And you were the one who said a coat makes it harder to look beautiful in that dress."

"Did I actually say that?"

"Yes." Tracy laughed. "I had to wonder who kidnapped my sister and replaced her with an imposter because you've never said anything like that before."

Polly sniffed.

"I do have someone in my life who sees me as beautiful. I want to live up to that."

"I think he's seen you at your worst and still he loves you. It's going to take a knock to the head to make him think otherwise."

There was a muffled noise coming from the seat next to them. Tracy looked up to see Morgan's shoulders shaking. It could have been from the shaking of the wagon as they headed along the street, but she was sure he was laughing.

It was so good to see her sister in such a happy relationship. Their marriage would be blessed. How could she get that for herself? Was it possible to talk to Thomas and escape the grips of Arnold Foster? Closing her eyes she whispered a prayer.

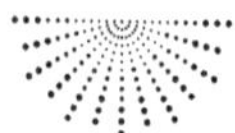

hen Tracy realized that they were going down the street where the courthouse was situated. Where Foster's offices were located. If Foster was in his office right now, he would be able to look out of the window and see them go past. Tracy wished Morgan had gone the other way, but this was the most direct route out of Jefferson City. Otherwise, they would put a lot more time into their journey and it was cold and silly to do so.

As if sensing her discomfort, Polly put her hand over Tracy's and gave them a squeeze.

"Don't look up, honey. You'll get yourself more upset."

"Is he looking?" Tracy whispered.

"No, but you will upset yourself if you start worrying about him again."

Polly was right, but it didn't stop Tracy from feeling awful. She felt like she was sneaking out after curfew, which was ridiculous. She was doing what she wanted for her Christmas Eve, and she wasn't about to bow down to a control freak. Tracy wanted to be with her friends, not with a man she despised.

"You two all right?" Morgan looked over his shoulder at them. "Sorry I had to go this way, but there wasn't really any avoiding it. I don't want you ladies catching a chill."

"We're fine," Polly assured him.

Tracy stared at Morgan.

"Why would you think I wouldn't be all right?" she asked.

"Well, we are going past Father's office." Morgan shrugged. "You're a grown woman, Tracy. Ignore him. He can't force you to be around him."

He knew? Of course, he knew. Tracy glared at Polly.

"I wish you hadn't told him about this."

"It is his father. And Morgan deserves to know what's going on, seeing as you are family now. Besides," Polly added as Tracy let out a sigh, "If I hadn't told him someone else would. Don't worry, he knows how to handle his father."

"I wouldn't say that," Morgan grunted. He had turned back to the horses, steering them in the direction of James's ranch. "But he doesn't dare argue with us. Me, especially. He knows I don't have any care to give him, especially after what he's done."

Tracy listened to this with a mixture of relief and confusion. Even in their worst moments, which had been a few towards the end, her own father was still loved. Tracy didn't think that would go away. To hear someone say that they had no feelings that were kind towards a parent was a little shocking.

"Was there a time when you actually loved him, Morgan?"

She didn't hear him, but his shoulders went up and down in a sigh.

"I'm sure there was. But the recent years have kind

of tainted everything." He barely glanced around, just concentrating on the way ahead. "Losing our mother changed him. We tried to help, to be sympathetic but it was no use. The man had always been hard and we weren't willing to hang around if he was going to be such a sour, controlling old man over it."

Tracy found herself realizing the irony of what Morgan had just said.

"You don't like to be controlled by him. And yet you're all getting married on Christmas Day at his insistence."

"What can I say? We're strange people."

"No comment," Polly said loudly, which elicited a laugh from Morgan.

They carried on in silence, Tracy huddling in her shawl with Polly holding her hand. She wasn't sure when they last had such a nerve-wracking drive. Morgan may have been good at his job, but he would certainly have been fired if he had been a coach driver. The wagon seemed to keep bouncing off the road, and Tracy was half-afraid they would be tipped out onto the road. They weren't that late, were they?

Finally, after what felt like forever, Morgan drew the wagon up outside the house. He pulled the horses to a halt and then jumped down from the seat, holding his hand up for them.

"Down you come, ladies. You have arrived."

"I've noticed," Polly grumbled as she took his hand. "I swear you were going to have us tipping over."

"You just don't appreciate me, my dear."

Polly was still grumbling as Morgan, who was laughing, helped Tracy out. Her legs felt a little wobbly and she swayed, but she stayed upright. Even though her heart was still racing from that ride, she managed to give Morgan a smile.

"Thanks for... escorting us."

"Anytime, Tracy." He glanced past her towards Polly. "You two go on inside. I'll put the horses away and then come join you."

"Don't be too long." Polly gave her future husband a big smile and swatted his arm. "Otherwise, James will be thinking that we got lost."

"I'm going to ignore that insinuation about my

driving." Morgan kissed her head and nudged Polly towards the door. "In you go. It gets colder up here at this time. Best you go in and get warm."

That sounded like a very good idea to Tracy. Taking Polly's hand, she headed into the house. The front door opened right into the living room, where it seemed like the whole of Jefferson City were congregating. It took a moment for Tracy to realize that it was just her friends and the Foster brothers.

Nicola was sitting on the couch with Shelley, baby Oliver curled up on Shelley's lap happily playing with a soft toy. Nicola's soon-to-be stepdaughter, Linda, was sitting on the floor playing with Tamsin, Anne's daughter. Jacira was with them, showing them a trick using her hands that had the girls enraptured.

Anne herself was standing by the fire, leaning into her groom, Chris, with his arm around her waist as he talked to his brother, Adam. Ernest and James were at the far end of the room talking in low whispers, but every so often Ernest was glancing over at Jacira. It was such a sweet look, something Tracy had not expected from Ernest, and her heart melted at the sight. Even with his adamant stance on not letting his father take charge, Ernest hadn't let that stop him from finally coming to terms with the fact Jacira was the woman he wanted in his life. At least one of the brothers had found a woman that was outside of their father's control. The rest were now engaged to the women that Thomas had been forced to bring here. He was an intuitive man and he had matched them all well.

Tracy smiled, pleased for Jacira, Ernest, and herself. She didn't think she could manage being a doctor's wife.

The only one she couldn't see who should be present was Matt. Polly had explained that Matt had the saloon shut for Christmas Day, but he couldn't do it for Christmas Eve, so Nicola and Linda were having Christmas dinner with Matt's family while he worked. Tracy had wondered why he didn't let the staff deal with it, but Polly said it was just Matt all over, he looked after his staff as if they were his family.

Tracy's heart stumbled. There were two other men here, standing near the couch. One, a middle-aged man with silver hair joining in the conversation with Nicola and Shelley. The other, a tall handsome man in his thirties with sun-kissed skin. He stood beside him, looking like he was involved but not including himself. Though he was there smiling and nodding, part of the group but, at the same time, keeping himself separate.

Thomas was here. Tracy's pulse skipped. She hadn't expected him to be here. Nobody had said anything. For a moment, she couldn't move. Her feet were rooted to the spot, and it was suddenly a lot warmer.

"Tracy?" Polly gently shook her arm. "Tracy, what's wrong?"

"I..."

Tracy's mouth went dry as Thomas looked around and their eyes met. They seemed to flash, and Tracy shivered. Why did she have to feel like this? Her feelings towards the man had grown, yes, but now she was beginning to feel like an eighteen-year-old girl in the first flushes of love. Awkward, very awkward, and feeling like she was making a fool of herself.

That hadn't happened before. Tracy had thought she could cope with Thomas's presence before, and she had. What had changed?

What's changed is that you have another man wanting you as his wife, and you're beginning to come to terms with the fact that you're going to have to tell Thomas what you want. It is the simple fear of rejection.

Thomas crossed to her. He certainly looked very fine, freshly shaven and in his black suit. Tracy was not petite, by any standards, but Thomas simply towered over her. He stopped before her and his eyes drifted over her face, a slight smile twitching at his mouth.

"Miss Brown."

That deep voice was like music to Tracy's ears. She loved to hear him talk. It was why she had ended up going to service more since moving away from home. Tracy just wanted to listen to him, even if the sermon sometimes went over her head. As long as she heard his voice she was happy.

Then she realized she was staring at him. Tracy gulped and shuffled from foot to foot, wishing that her face wasn't going red.

"Pastor Thomas. I... I didn't know you were going to be here."

"Initially, we weren't, but then James said he wanted us to be here, so we thought 'why not'."

"We?" Then Tracy recognized the silver-haired man moving around the couch and coming towards them with a welcoming smile. "Oh, Pastor Michael."

"Miss Brown." Michael gave Tracy a bow before bowing to Polly. "Miss Brown. You two are looking lovely tonight."

Polly was laughing as she shook her head.

"Honestly, Pastor Michael, there are times when I wonder if you're really a confirmed bachelor. You behave like an incorrigible rogue at times."

Michael's eyes twinkled as he regarded Polly.

"Maybe in a past life. But I assure you, now, it is just all flowery words from me."

Tracy laughed. She liked Michael Davis. He was a warm, generous man. He had been a frequent visitor to Thomas's home, and he had been just as welcoming towards her. Tracy felt comfortable with him, even if she was aware of Michael giving her and Thomas knowing looks when he thought she wasn't watching.

"There you two are."

Tracy turned to see James walking towards them. He kissed her cheek before kissing Polly's, giving her a frown.

"You may be marrying my brother, Polly, but you still work here. You were supposed to be helping Amy in the kitchen."

"I was!" Polly protested. "Amy practically shoved me out and told me to get ready myself. If something's happened, it's because I was doing as I was told!"

"Hmm," James grunted. But his eyes were twinkling with humor. "Well, dinner will be ready in a moment. If it isn't very nice, don't be mean to her, please?"

Tracy put a finger to her lips.

Michael chuckled. "I'll not say a word."

"I'm sure Amy's dinner will be just fine, James." Thomas clapped James on the shoulder. "Don't worry about your future bride so much. She's far more capable than you think."

"Even so..."

"Come on, now."

Thomas steered James away. Tracy watched them go. Thomas was one of those people who could put people at ease just by talking to them. He was shy and reserved, but he knew when to assert himself. For the most part.

Tracy just wished he could assert himself in her current situation. She needed the help right now.

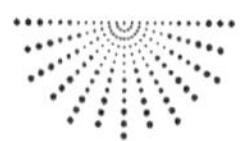

CHAPTER FIVE

Even though Thomas knew that Tracy was going to be there, his heart had missed a few beats when he saw her enter the room. She did look incredibly lovely in that red dress, the same shade as her hair. That magnificent hair was coiled up on her head, revealing a long, delicate neck he hadn't realized she had. Then again, he hadn't seen her dress up as nicely as this.

It was all he could do to stop staring. Even when they were face to face, beyond the pleasantries, Thomas couldn't find anything to say. He was just mesmerized.

It didn't help when they went in to dinner, to a table

so long Thomas didn't think a table like it existed. He ended up sitting across from Tracy, who was seated between Michael and Ernest.

Ernest was in a convivial mood, and he was happily talking to everyone, although he did keep an eye on Jacira. His bride sat between him and Thomas and Thomas noticed that she was decidedly nervous when they first sat down. Even though she knew everyone and she was well-liked, she was still scared. Understandably so, since Thomas knew the Foster brothers could be a bit much when in the same room. However, they all made her so welcome, and luckily, she loosened up through dinner and was interacting as much as everyone else.

Tracy certainly seemed to be enjoying herself. The tension that had been in her shoulders when she first arrived had now gone. She was sitting across from him with a warm smile, laughing at the terrible jokes and joining in with the conversation. Thomas had seen her ability to charm a room before, and this time was no different. Tracy was just a warm person everyone wanted to be around.

She certainly seemed to be enjoying her time talking

to Pastor Michael. The older man had turned the charm on her and they engaged in a conversation that made Thomas's stomach tighten into knots. He wanted to be the person who engaged Tracy in such a way, and yet his friend and mentor was in that position. It did make him wonder, yet again, if Michael was as confirmed a bachelor as he claimed to be; he had far too much charm and smooth ability talking to a woman than was comfortable for Thomas.

But Tracy did keep looking over at him. She snuck glances at him, and when Thomas caught those glances they held each other's gaze for a moment longer than necessary. Then Tracy would give him a sweet smile before turning back to focus on Michael. That made him feel a warm glow in his chest, but he still wished he was able to talk to her as he used to. They could talk about pretty much anything before. Why was he struggling now?

Because you're scared you're going to lose her. And you don't want to mess it up.

When dinner was finished, everyone started moving into the drawing room at the back of the house.

Thomas felt stuffed; that food had been delicious. Considering Amy had spent most of the afternoon doing it almost single-handedly, it was certainly a good spread. Amy had been blushing with pride all the way through dinner as everyone complimented her, Thomas included. James had certainly picked a good one there if Amy could cook that well for so many people.

There was a lot more to Amy Growcott than being good at cooking, but it was certainly something she excelled at.

Thomas wasn't sure if he could sit around watching Tracy talk to Michael. It was like he was monopolizing her time, and Thomas wasn't confident enough to go over there and tell him that he was cutting in. Instead, he headed outside, stepping into the chilly air. It was darker than when he had first arrived, and it was very much colder. Being higher up than Jefferson City, the air tended to be cooler when the weather headed towards winter. Their area could have very mild winters, but they were unpredictable. One day could be warm, almost humid, and the next could be threatening snow. It was odd, and Thomas had given up guessing what the weather was going to do ages ago. But he wouldn't have it any other way.

He just wished that he could keep this a little longer. But Thomas knew it wouldn't last. Not if Arnold Foster had anything to do with it. He would make sure Thomas was out of the town by the New Year by any means necessary. Just because he refused to make Tracy go to him.

Thomas couldn't do that, not in all good conscience.

"Thomas?"

Thomas looked around. Tracy was in the doorway, regarding him with a slight frown. Thomas hadn't heard her come out.

"Tracy. I..." Dear Lord, why did he have to sound like a fool now? "Are you not enjoying your evening?"

"I'm having a great time. Things are fine." Tracy stepped out onto the porch, her frown softening as she gave him a placid smile. "What about you?"

"It's been hosted really well." Thomas meant it. "Amy and James have impressed me."

"If that's the case, why are you out here?"

"I... I just needed some air." And to resist the urge to snatch Tracy away from Michael. He really was laying it on thick. Thomas looked over her shoulder, seeing the movement of the other guests in the drawing room. They were, effectively, alone. He should go back inside or have someone close by to witness them. But Thomas found himself not wanting to move. He just wanted a bit of time with Tracy, alone. Away from everyone else. It was going to get a lot of raised eyebrows, but Michael had said there were times when people needed to be selfish.

Thomas wanted to be selfish, just this once.

Tracy wrapped her arms around her middle and shivered.

"I didn't realize it would be so cold up here. Polly warned me it would be chilly, but not like this."

"The weather's very deceptive here." Thomas shrugged out of his jacket. The cold whipped through his thin shirt, but he ignored his own shivering and draped it over Tracy's shoulders. "Here."

"Thank you."

The smile Tracy gave him was worth the cold. She slipped her arms into his sleeves and seemed to huddle into his jacket. It looked huge on her, practically swamping her, but Thomas couldn't take his eyes off her as Tracy turned up the collar and gathered it around her face for a moment, closing her eyes, taking a breath. Was she sniffing his collar? Thomas cleared his throat and looked away.

"Tomorrow's going to be busy." Why did he have to start talking about the weddings? Too late now. "A little too busy, I think. I've never married so many people in one day."

"I'm sure you'll be fine," Tracy said. "You're good at working under pressure. And working out of what you consider comfortable."

"You really think that?"

"I do."

Thomas had never heard anyone say that to him before. Tracy had a lot more faith in him than he realized. He shoved his hands into his pockets. Even with the pressure, tomorrow was going to be difficult anyway, and not just because of the weddings. Thomas would be looking at Tracy and wishing he was brave enough to admit that he loved her.

If it hadn't been for the situation, and Foster's loud declaration of claiming Tracy, Thomas would have said something long ago. He knew this would have been discussed and he could have married Tracy a long time ago if knowing she was chosen for someone else hadn't got in the way.

She was chosen for someone. You. You just took a little too long in realizing it.

"Polly looks beautiful in her dress," Tracy said. She was staring out across the orchard that wrapped around the side of the house. "I don't think I've seen her look so radiant."

"Knowing what she's like, I'm surprised she stayed still long enough for you to help her out with the alterations."

"She is a lively person."

"And a wriggly one."

Tracy laughed. Her eyes seemed to be sparkling now. That hadn't happened while she had been talking to

Michael, Thomas realized. The real Tracy had been subdued. This was the real Tracy Brown. The one who was more vibrant when she was around him.

Foster would break that. He didn't like women to have their own thoughts without his input.

"Are you going to be doing more matchmaking after this, or is this it?" Tracy asked. She brushed her hair out of her eyes. Thomas wanted to do that for her, but he kept his hands firmly in his pockets.

"Oh, no! No more matchmaking for me." Thomas shook his head. "This was by force, and it was too much of a headache. Far too many rules and stipulations. Far too much wondering if I was going to have a heart attack due to the stress Foster put me under. That's it for me."

"Even though you've been successful?"

"Not quite successful." Thomas glanced at her. "I didn't get all the women married."

Tracy shrugged. She looked better in his jacket than he did.

"I can't compete with Jacira. She's a beautiful woman and it was clear to everyone that Ernest was mad about her. While I think Ernest is a good man, I don't think I could cope with being married to a doctor. Not with the hours he keeps." Tracy adjusted the sleeves of his jacket. "Jacira's better suited for him."

Thomas couldn't argue with that. He watched as Tracy walked to the end of the porch, leaning on the wooden railing as she looked out over the apple trees. She looked troubled, almost sad. Was she worried about Foster? Thomas certainly was. He knew he should go back inside, but he didn't want to leave her. He walked over and leaned on the railing beside her.

"Do you think you'll ever marry?" he asked.

"I... I don't know. It depends on what happens, I suppose. Things are just..." Tracy looked up and paused, staring up at something above their heads.

"Just what?"

"Do you realize what we're standing under?"

Thomas looked up. Just above his head, tied to the rafters, was a generous sprig of mistletoe. Thomas was surprised he hadn't seen it.

"What's mistletoe doing out here?"

"Don't you know what happens under the mistletoe?"

"Of course, I do…" Thomas felt his face getting warm. "But it's a bit of an obscure place to put it."

"And not the only one." Tracy's smile was sly. "I've seen them dotted around the house. It's almost like the Foster boys want an excuse to kiss their future wives."

"I see." The thought of Tracy being caught under the mistletoe for a kiss by anyone else, even in innocence, didn't sit well with Thomas at all. "Have you been caught under it yet?"

Tracy was silent for a brief moment. Then she pushed off the railing and tugged Thomas down by his shirt, rising up on her tiptoes.

"Not until now," she whispered against his mouth.

Thomas didn't want to push her away as she kissed him. He heard a groan and realized it was coming from him. He kissed her back, his arms slipping around her to pull her close. Tracy made an approving sound in her throat and her arms went around his neck. With their different heights, it was a little awkward, but Thomas didn't care. He finally had Tracy where he wanted her.

This should have happened a long time ago, but what now?

CHAPTER SIX

For an initial moment, Tracy thought she had ruined it, that Thomas was going to push her away. Instead, he had growled in a way that made his chest vibrate under her hands, and then he was kissing her back. Whoa, she had certainly unleashed something in him. The normally placid, collected man had been holding back. And she liked it.

A lot.

She should have taken the reins months ago and kissed him, but the fear of rejection was always there. This time, no rejection. Just complete acceptance.

Thomas broke the kiss, resting his forehead against

hers. It shouldn't have worked with the awkward angle, but this simple gesture somehow made her feel safe, cared for, loved.

"I'm such a coward."

Tracy blinked.

"Why do you say that?"

"Because it takes a stupid piece of greenery to get the courage to kiss you."

Tracy smiled and kissed him.

"Me too... you didn't need to worry... and don't you dare stop now."

"I don't want to." Thomas's arms tightened around her. "I just wish I had managed this to start with, instead of letting everything..."

"Stop talking." Tracy dragged his head down. "Just. Stop. Talking."

She had finally gotten the courage to do this and she wasn't going to waste it by talking. Thomas made an approving noise as he kissed her again, his hand cupping her head. Tracy could feel the pins coming loose and her hair starting to slip free, but she didn't care. She had gotten what she had wanted for a long time. Her hair wasn't as important.

Not right now.

"What is going on here?"

Thomas broke the kiss so abruptly that Tracy was practically gasping air. His arms tightened around her, and then she saw Thomas glaring at someone over her head. Then Tracy heard the voice again, the one that made her heart sink. She looked over her shoulder and saw Arnold Foster storming up onto the porch, a look of fury on his face. A horse was tethered to the well. They had been so engrossed in their embrace, neither of them had heard someone arriving. Everyone was here, and Foster was certainly not invited.

From the look of it, he had seen everything.

Foster stormed over to them, practically baring his teeth.

"What's the meaning of this, Brooks?"

"It's a kiss under the mistletoe, Mayor Foster." Why did those words sting? But Thomas didn't remove his arms from Tracy. "We're consenting adults."

"Consenting?" Foster snorted rudely. "It didn't look like just a kiss from what I saw."

Why was he even here? Had he actually seen them? Tracy wanted to go back inside. Thomas fixed Foster with a hard stare.

"I didn't realize you were invited here, sir. Your sons said you weren't going to be a guest. They wanted it to be a happy occasion."

"I saw Morgan driving past with Tracy on board earlier. I knew then she wouldn't be coming over to my home tonight." Foster looked at Tracy with disappointment in his eyes. "I'm here to take her. Now, you take your hands off my woman."

Anger flared inside Tracy. Foster was treating her like a piece of property and she was not having it. Now she knew that Thomas was not pushing her away, Tracy was more than prepared to release the claws. She looked up at Thomas and touched his jaw.

"Let me talk to him," she whispered.

"No." Thomas shook his head. "I'm not just going to leave you alone with him."

"You're not." Tracy kissed his jaw. "Get one of the brothers and then stay out of sight. He tries to take me with him, you can step in. But don't worry, I'm not going anywhere willingly."

Thomas still didn't look convinced, but he did release her, albeit reluctantly. Giving Tracy's hand a kiss, he headed back inside. Hopefully, he would be back within moments with backup. Tracy didn't want to be alone with Foster, but she wasn't about to bring him inside. She could handle a couple of minutes.

Just.

Foster was scowling at her.

"I thought better of you, Miss Brown. I don't like the sight of you in the arms of another man."

"Having a kiss under the mistletoe does not constitute a bad thing. And I have no obligations to anyone. Who I kiss, under the mistletoe or not, is none of your business."

"Stop that! You're about to become my bride. I'm not about to have you kissing other people."

That had to be the worst proposal Tracy had ever

heard. It was more of a statement of fact, and it made Tracy really angry.

"Become your bride?" she cried. "When did I agree to that?"

"If you know what's good for you, you'll become my wife. If not you will suffer..."

"And then you just threatened me."

Foster sighed and stepped towards her. Tracy backed away, keeping space between them and trying not to back up against the railing. She didn't want to be pinned in.

"You know it's the right thing to do." Foster was talking to her like a child. "And Pastor Brooks will not be officiating our wedding. He'll be banned from it all and I'll have someone else marry us. I can't have him trying to take you during our wedding vows."

"What about taking my opinion into account? What about asking if I actually want to marry you? Because the answer will be no, no matter how many times you pester me about it."

Foster sighed and approached her. Tracy backed away again, bumping into the railing. She darted away, managing to get around Foster and nearer the door. If she could just run in and slam the door on him, that would be good. James would understand; he was adamant about his father never crossing the threshold.

"Come on, Tracy." Foster was beginning to pout now that he realized he wasn't getting his own way. "You know it's going to happen."

"No, I don't," Tracy snapped. "The idea of a marriage is that the husband and wife are supposed to actually like each other, even if just a little bit. Preferably, they love each other. I don't even like you! You make my skin crawl. You've been pestering me for months; surely, you should have gotten the message... if not, here it is again, I don't want anything to do with you!"

"But I adore you," Foster protested. Now he sounded like a child not getting his favorite toy. "Isn't that enough? I can give you anything. I can make things easy for your friends or I can make them difficult. Be sensible and make the right choice, you'll come to love me in the end."

"No, I won't. Not after the way you've treated your

sons, after how you've treated Thomas." Tracy shook her head. "No... never."

There was a movement just over Foster's shoulder, and Tracy saw Thomas return. Morgan was with him. Both men loomed in the doorway, Thomas's expression was one of fury and Morgan looked like he wanted to throttle his father. Tracy caught Morgan's eye and shot him a look. Stay back, she was handling this.

Foster pursed his lips. If he had been expecting Tracy to agree to everything because she was normally an easygoing, placid woman, he had severely underestimated her. Poke the bear long enough and they're going to fight back. Tracy had had enough.

"I have a right to talk to my sons how I wish," Foster hissed. "They are my children. As for the pastor... well, he's nothing. He'll amount to nothing... not in this town. I doubt he'll even have a job much longer."

That made Tracy feel sick. Her anger was burning more. But before she could respond to him, Thomas's voice made her jump. He stepped onto the porch and squared up to Foster. Being over a foot taller than the older man, it didn't take much for Foster to falter.

"You think that I'm nothing, Mayor Foster? You really think that?"

"I do think that." How Foster still had bravado despite being stood up to by someone much bigger than him, Tracy had no idea. "You're never going to be good enough for Tracy, and you're never going to have her in your life because she's mine. Nobody takes away my woman."

"Your woman?" Tracy cried. "Stop saying that, I'm not your woman!"

Thomas looked like he wanted to take a swing at Foster. Instead, he shook his head with a scowl.

"This is disgusting behavior from you, Foster. Just disgusting."

"How dare you?"

"How dare I? How dare you assume things are going to be what you want. I should have turned you down when you demanded I find wives for your children. It was not your responsibility to find them wives, nor was it mine, but you made my life awful. You blackmailed me, threatened me, threatened the women if I didn't help. I felt like I had no choice." Thomas's hands were clenched at his side. "I'm not doing it anymore. You've pushed me too much, and I won't have it. Not when it comes to Tracy."

Tracy had never seen Thomas look so angry before. From the look on his face, neither had Morgan. He was staring at Thomas like a perfect stranger had just walked into their lives. Foster looked a little startled that someone was actually standing up to him.

"How your sons ended up being well-rounded human beings when you're their parent, I have no idea," Thomas went on. "You should be happy that they are successful and have their own lives, but you just want to control them. Even to the point of arranging marriages for them."

"It worked, didn't it?" Foster snapped. "They're all getting married now."

"And you're not going to get any credit for that, Father," Morgan said sharply. He folded his arms. "We will not be looking at you and think of you as the person who saved our lives by finding us a woman to marry. We see you as a meddler, which you are. You're not going to bring us back into line just by doing something that would have happened sooner or later."

From the look of shock that passed over his face, Tracy gathered that Foster had not expected this outburst towards him. He was used to getting things done his way, and his sons didn't speak to him enough to shut him down each and every time. Morgan looked like he wanted to say more, but he also looked ready to explode.

How badly did you have to mess up as a parent so your own children didn't care for you?

"At least something came out of it." Foster turned to Tracy, his expression softening. "Tracy, come here. I wasn't thinking about marriage after your mother died, Morgan, because no one would be able to match up to her. Then I met Tracy, she can easily match her and then some."

Tracy found herself reacting on instinct. She had been itching to do this for a while, but his words made her snap. She stepped forward and slapped him. The sound made her ears ring; it was really loud.

Thomas and Morgan were now looking bewildered, and Foster had frozen. He really hadn't expected her to hit him.

"Get this into your head, Mayor Foster." Tracy was practically snarling. "I will never marry you and I will declare it to the heavens that I don't wish to have anything to do with you. Don't even think about approaching me again, Mayor, because I will scream and make sure everyone is aware of what sort of man you are. Don't threaten my friends with ruin or I will turn things around and ruin you."

She had to get out of there, otherwise, she was going to lash out again. The sight of Foster was making her blood boil. Stepping around Foster as far as she could, Tracy went straight to Thomas. He pulled her into his embrace immediately, his arms tightening as she buried her face against his chest.

Tracy was shaking, wishing that Foster would just leave. He was not going to let this go. It didn't matter what her answer was, Foster was going to keep coming back until she said yes. That was not going to happen, but Tracy was going to lose her mind if she had to keep dealing with him.

"Take Tracy inside, Thomas," Morgan said quietly. "And then get my brothers. We'll deal with Father."

"You will not be dealing with me like that!" Foster snarled. "Have some respect for your father!"

"Like you had respect for us?" Morgan snapped back. "You've already pushed us away with your actions, Father. Don't make this worse on yourself."

That was the last thing Tracy heard before she was taken inside.

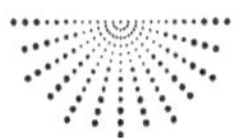

CHAPTER SEVEN

Thomas was shaking after what happened. Foster had come out to them to cause trouble and take Tracy away. No matter how many times she said no, he just rolled his eyes and treated her like a child. Thomas couldn't believe that he would be that thick-headed to even believe he would get his own way.

He was just glad that Tracy was away from him. Foster wouldn't set foot in the house if James and his brothers had anything to do with it. As of now, they were all outside and there was a lot of shouting. Thomas had looked out of the window a few times and saw Morgan and Chris leading Foster towards his horse with James untying the reins from the well.

Foster was fighting to stay off the horse, shouting loudly that he wasn't going anywhere. Then Ernest came out of the stables across the yard with another horse, saddled up and ready. Eventually, Morgan was on one horse and Foster was on the other. He was still protesting loudly as they tried to get him to mount, so James and Chris had pinned him to the ground and tied his hands behind his back before tying his ankles together, throwing him over the back of the horse like a lump of meat. It would have been amusing if it wasn't also sad.

A grown man should never need his adult sons to treat him like a spoiled child. It was the wrong way around, and it wasn't a good look for the town's mayor.

At least he was going. Morgan grabbed the reins of Foster's horse and led his father out of the yard. Even with the doors closed, Thomas could still hear the shouts.

He turned away from the window and went over to Tracy. She had been urged to sit by the fire, Thomas's jacket was still around her shoulders. The women had fussed over her when she came in - everyone had heard the shouting - but once Tracy was sitting down and staring into the flames, they left her be. Polly was the last to go, giving Thomas a meaningful look before she left the room.

Thomas didn't need to be smart to know what she was trying to convey. She wanted her sister taken care of. Thomas was more than happy to do that if Tracy wanted him there. If their kiss was anything to go by, she did.

Tracy looked up as Thomas approached her, giving him a small smile.

"Hey."

"Hey. They're gone now. Foster looks like a trussed-up turkey on the back of his horse."

"Trussed up turkey?"

"They had to tie him up to get him going home."

Tracy bit her lip, her expression saying she wanted to laugh but she was holding back. She swallowed and looked away.

"That was so embarrassing. I didn't think it would go that badly," she said in almost a whisper.

"You stood up for yourself, which is admirable."

"And you stood up for me." Tracy's smile widened a little. "Thank you."

Thomas felt his chest squeezing. He was lost! Even after their kiss, why was this so difficult? He sat beside her on the couch, staring into the fire before them.

"Foster's going to make sure I'm out of here by the New Year," he said quietly. "I'll be looking for a new place."

"He can't do that, can he? Everyone loves you."

"It only takes one small but vicious rumor to circulate and be believed. Then I'll be forced out. It doesn't matter if we find who starts it, all that matters is how it manifests. Then Foster gets his own way."

And the rumor would manifest, especially if it was juicy. The townspeople of Jefferson City meant well, but they would be fascinated by a salacious lie. They wouldn't care if it was a lie, by the time it was revealed. As long as it gave them a talking point. Foster was petty enough to do that.

"We can say that it's a lie..." Tracy began, but Thomas shook his head.

"It won't matter. My career will be ruined here. I'm just going to have to pack and make arrangements."

Michael would help him out. He had done so before, and would certainly lend a hand now. Thomas didn't want to leave, but he would if he had to. He could just hope that he could persuade Tracy to come with him. If he could get the courage to ask her.

You've just kissed her and you're getting scared now?

"Well, let me know when you leave," Tracy said. "Because I'm coming with you."

Thomas felt the tightness in his chest lessening. But even then, he still had his doubts. His confidence was really not there when he needed it.

"You've just settled here, Tracy. I don't want to upend your life with you following me. I don't even know where I'm going yet."

"I don't care about how settled I am." Tracy put her hand on his arm. "Just as long as I'm with you."

"Tracy..."

"No, Thomas. You do not do that to me after what we just did." Tracy turned on the couch to face him, fixing him still with the fiery expression in her eyes. "I'm not having you tell me that it's not a good idea. Do you have any idea how much courage it took for me to kiss you even with the mistletoe? I've wanted to do that for months, and I always back out because I was sure you would turn me down. Now I've managed to do it, I'm not going to give up on you... not now."

Thomas stared. That confession he had not been expecting.

"You've wanted to kiss me for months?"

"Yes." Tracy cupped his jaw. "I fell in love with you a long time ago. Through your letters, even when you were meant to be the one procuring wives. It's part of the reason I said I would help you with putting my friends with the Foster brothers, just to spend time with you. I always felt warm and safe when I was with you. I don't want to lose that now you're planning to leave."

She loved him. Thomas had been hoping for that declaration, but he had been too scared to go looking for it.

"Tracy." He sagged against the cushions. "You're far too good for me."

"I was going to say the same of you." Tracy's eyes searched his face. "I never will marry Foster, no matter what he wants. I love you, and that's not going to change because he wants it his own way."

He had to admire her strength there. He wrapped an arm around her shoulders and tugged her close. Tracy went willingly, leaning into his side as Thomas put his arms around her. It felt really good to do that. Thomas was feeling warmer and lighter the more they poured their hearts out.

Well, Thomas hadn't done that, yet. But he would.

"In my dreams, you said that you loved me," Thomas said as he stared at the fire. "But I never heard it when I was awake. Those dreams made me smile, made me glad that you chose to spend time with me instead of anyone else."

"What are you trying to say?"

"This." Thomas kissed her forehead, brushing her hair away from her face. "I fell for you months ago, Tracy.

Pretty much as soon as you came into the room. But you were meant to be a woman promised for one of Foster's sons. I couldn't intrude on that, not when Foster was watching me and with that blackmail hanging over my head. For a year now, ever since we first started exchanging letters, I wished I could find myself a wife who was like you. Who was the support I needed, who made me feel better just by being present." His arms tightened. "Then when Foster said he was going to marry you, I was so angry. But even then, I couldn't bring myself to confess my feelings. I thought... I thought you would believe I was doing it as an obligation."

"I know you're not like that." Tracy looked up at him. "You should have said something before, though."

"Maybe you should have kissed me before."

Tracy swatted his shoulder with a groan. Thomas chuckled and kissed her. He was feeling better. Much better, in fact. Perhaps he could sweeten this a little more with something else? Could he?

Absolutely.

"Do you think you could manage being married to a pastor?" he asked. "It's not exactly a vibrant life."

"I can manage plain and simple. I prefer it." Tracy shook her head. "And you need to work more on your eloquence skills."

"I love you, Tracy, I love you more than I thought possible, will you marry me?"

Tracy kissed him once more and then whispered her yes against his lips.

"Wow, after that kiss I think marriage is just a formality."

Tracy laughed.

"I suppose. When were you thinking?"

Thomas had a good date in mind.

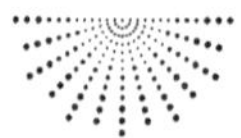

"I can't believe you actually managed to pull that off," Tracy said as she leaned into Thomas's side. "That was quite impressive."

Thomas beamed. Tracy hadn't seen him this happy before.

"Michael said it wouldn't take much to add one more set of vows onto the end. Although, I have to admit even I was surprised he could make it look so effortless." He shuddered. "I'm glad I wasn't doing the ceremonies. I would certainly have messed it up."

There was a laugh behind them and Tracy turned. Morgan had stepped out of Thomas's house and was walking across the grass towards them, two glasses in his hands. He handed one to each of them.

"Another drink for the extra bride and groom. And to respond to what you just said, Thomas, you wouldn't have messed up. You're the most unruffled man I know, and that's saying something."

Tracy giggled.

"That really is saying something."

Thomas blushed. It was sweet to see him bashful. It hadn't even been twenty-four hours since they had agreed to get married, and Tracy was finding this relaxed, more confident side of Thomas endearing. But his modesty was still there and it was adorable to her.

When he had said they would be getting married with her sister and their friends, Tracy had thought he was being silly. It was such short notice, and she didn't even have a dress. But Thomas got busy, and an hour before the ceremony the local seamstress had turned up with a dress from her store in a fabulous champagne color. It was a perfect winter dress that could easily double as a wedding dress, such a beautiful garment. Tracy was still in awe that she had been permitted to wear it for free, that it was a gift for her. That lady was worth her weight in gold.

Nobody seemed to bat an eyelid that Thomas and Tracy were joining the line of brides and grooms at the church. Nobody said anything and Michael barely missed a beat as he married them as well. Then Tracy realized Thomas had organized everything, told everyone what he was doing, and they had fitted right in. This was the quickest engagement Tracy had ever heard of, and it ended up being the least stressful event in her life. Thomas had taken care of it all without thought. She couldn't thank him enough for that.

She was aware that part of the reason for marrying so quickly was to prevent Arnold Foster from protesting about it and trying to get it annulled or made void. But Chris had put his deputies outside and had orders not to let Foster in. It was a relief to know they were going to be undisturbed.

Now they were at Thomas's house for the reception, and Tracy and Thomas had been taking a moment to themselves out in the garden. To Tracy's surprise, it had been snowing and there was a light dusting of it across the garden. According to Thomas, it wasn't often that it snowed on Christmas day, so this was something to be treasured.

"You certainly know how to put things together regardless of everything else, Thomas," Morgan added. "You're the driving force behind it all, and we do appreciate it."

"Even with the way it all started out?" Thomas queried.

"Even then." Morgan shrugged. "This isn't a credit to Father, even if he forcibly put a fire under you. This is a credit to you."

Tracy could tell how much that meant to her husband. He had been worried about how this would affect him with regards to his friendships with the Foster brothers, but he needn't have worried. They were stubborn and could be angry, but they wouldn't have blamed him. Not when they had new brides out of it.

"Don't expect me to do it on a regular basis, though," Thomas warned as he took a hefty swig of his drink. "Six - seven - matches in a year is enough for me."

Morgan chuckled.

"I'm sure you'll be changing your mind in a couple of days." Then his laughter faded and he frowned. "I overheard Tracy and Polly a short while ago. You're not thinking of leaving Jefferson City, are you?"

Tracy winced. She had only confided this to Polly, her confidant as well as her sister. Nobody else was supposed to know beyond Pastor Michael, who had already agreed to help them out. Thomas glanced at her before turning to Morgan, slipping an arm around his wife.

"Your father is going to make sure I get driven out. It's best to head him off and leave first."

But Morgan was already shaking his head before Thomas had finished speaking.

"That's not going to happen. Not with us standing up to him."

Tracy wasn't surprised at this - Polly had already told her Morgan and his brothers would do this - but Thomas's expression said he was surprised.

"You're going to go toe-to-toe with your father... for me?"

"Of course, you are our friend and family now. We do it often. This won't be any different." Morgan reached out and clasped Thomas's shoulder. "And we're not going to let him drive you out of town because he's throwing a tantrum over a badly bruised ego. We want you to stay here, and it's going to happen."

Thomas looked like someone had hit him over the head. Tracy wrapped her arm around his waist and hugged him close, looking up at Morgan.

"What if a rumor starts going around about Thomas? What if people believe it?"

"Those with common sense will know that it's wrong." Morgan sounded very sure of it. "And those who do believe it will have the six of us telling them otherwise. Add our wives in, and we'll be a force to be reckoned with. Our family is very strong when we bond together."

"Even if it's against the family patriarch," Tracy added.

"Self-proclaimed patriarch," Morgan reiterated. "We don't ever talk about him like that."

"I..." Thomas still looked dazed. Tracy wondered if he had ever had so many people standing up for him before. "I don't know what to say, Morgan?"

Morgan arched an eyebrow.

"You really think we wouldn't stand up for a friend? Someone who is also now family?"

"People have done worse in your position."

That made Tracy's heart ache. She reached up on tiptoe and kissed Thomas' cheek.

"You're lovable, that's why I'm marrying you, and that's why Morgan and his brothers love you."

"I wouldn't go that far," Morgan said with raised eyebrows in her direction, "but it's close enough."

Thomas cleared his throat and used his glass to cover his mouth, but Tracy could see that he was smiling.

"I think I understand the sentiment, Morgan. And I still don't know what to say."

Morgan smiled. Tracy could see why Polly had fallen for him. That smile, when it was relaxed, was devastating.

"You don't have to say anything, Thomas. You did something you didn't want to do, but it turned out well. You brought all of us someone we love. Now we're returning the favor to help you out. And I don't think Polly would forgive me if I let her sister leave without helping to fight for her."

That sounded like Polly, all right. Tracy stepped forward and kissed Morgan's cheek.

"You're sweeter than you make yourself out to be, Morgan."

"Just don't tell anyone that." Morgan winked at her before turning back to Thomas. "Don't worry about it, Thomas. We're going to make sure you don't go anywhere."

Tracy watched the oldest Foster brother walk away. Morgan was a mixed bag of emotions, and his softer side was often kept at bay. She had noticed that when she first met him and had decided he would be a good temperament for Polly. Her sister would thank her for it one day.

She turned back to Thomas, who was still looking slightly bewildered.

"Do you think it'll really happen?" she asked.

"If there's one thing I know about the Foster family is that they're stubborn." Thomas smiled as he sipped his drink. "You think Arnold Foster is bad enough? His sons were cut from the same cloth with that attitude. They can push right back twice as hard."

"I hope so." Tracy approached her husband and took his hand. "Even though I would follow you anywhere, I don't want you to leave. This is your home."

"It is." Thomas's expression softened. He raised her hand to his lips and kissed her fingers. "I love you."

"And I love you." Tracy glanced over her shoulder at the house. It was full of the six other couples, the pastor, and a few close friends and family. "Are we going to join everyone else?"

"In a bit." Thomas smiled and linked his fingers with hers, tugging her down the path. "I want a bit of quiet time with you first. Maybe a walk to the end of the garden and back again?"

Tracy liked the sound of that.

"Pastor Brooks."

Thomas looked up. And found himself freezing. Arnold Foster was walking across the street towards him, practically cornering Thomas at the gate of his house. Thomas debated going in and ignoring him, but his good nature wouldn't let him do it. And there was no chance of bringing Foster inside; Tracy was still settling in, and he didn't want her subjected to this man.

Taking a deep breath and squaring his shoulders, Thomas turned to Foster with a bland smile.

"Mayor Foster. Happy New Year."

"Happy New Year."

Foster stopped before him and hesitated. Something was not right about him. There was none of the confidence, the arrogance that Thomas was used to seeing. Instead, Foster was subdued, a little withdrawn. It was like his confidence had been sucked out of him. Thomas wasn't sure what to make of this. Was this a ploy to get Thomas back onside? Or was the man genuine? Thomas didn't know right now.

"Can I talk to you, Pastor?" Foster asked.

"It depends." Thomas folded his arms. "Do I need a witness to this?"

"No. I'm not going to push you into anything."

From the way things had happened between them, Thomas wasn't sure if that was true or not. The past week since their confrontation on Christmas Eve had been surprisingly quiet. Thomas had been looking over his shoulder expecting to see Foster turn up and attack him again while he was alone. Tracy was similarly skittish, but she seemed to have more faith in Morgan and his brothers and she was calmer by the day after Boxing Day. She kept him on an even keel, urging him to just take a deep breath and let Morgan deal with it.

Thomas would gladly let the Foster family take care of everything. What he wasn't expecting was for Foster to actually approach him, looking like he hadn't slept in a while and pretty much a shadow of his former self. That put Thomas on the back foot.

"I..." Foster looked at the ground, and then he looked up. "I wanted to apologize for what I've done."

It took a moment for Thomas to realize what he had just heard. He frowned.

"Did your sons put you up to this?"

"They've all spoken to me, I guess on Christmas Eve they did a bit more than speak. They told me to cut my act and behave like an adult. None of them told me to come here and apologize to you. In fact," Foster rubbed the back of his neck, "Chris told me specifically not to come to you and apologize for my actions."

Thomas found himself smiling.

"You still have to defy your son's wishes, don't you?"

"I can't give up a bad habit that easily." Foster's smile was brief and then it was gone. He took a deep breath. "Please, don't make this difficult for me. I'm struggling to swallow my pride here, and it's not easy."

Thomas waited. He was still surprised at Foster's apology. This was clearly not something he was good at. When did he learn how to own up for his mistakes?

"I'm sorry for forcing you to find women that my sons didn't want. I'm sorry for threatening your livelihood when things weren't going how I wanted them to." Foster grimaced. "I'm sorry for telling you to leave when I saw you with Miss Brown. And I'm sorry... for everything else." He shrugged. "The list will be far too long, and we'll be here all day, but those are the main things I'm very aware of."

Thomas let that sink in. The Christmas when Foster ordered him to find women for his sons had been a sad one, and Foster had been intimidating. Last Christmas, he had been terrifying. Now, he was different. Very different, and actually apologizing. As far as Thomas was aware, the man never apologized.

"I was not expecting any of that," he admitted.

"I like to keep people on their toes."

They shared a brief smile, which felt rather strange. Then Thomas frowned.

"Why the sudden turnaround? What's made you want to apologize? It can't have just been your sons telling you that you messed up."

"They yelled at me, and that I could take. It was..." Foster's face flushed and he looked away. "You know I wasn't permitted into the church on Christmas Day. Christopher's deputies made sure I couldn't get inside, so I waited across the street. I saw everyone coming out, and that was when I saw how happy my sons were. I hadn't seen them like that in a long time, not since before my wife died. I wanted to feel the joy and satisfaction that I had managed to make this happen for them, but I couldn't. I just felt lost. It hit me then that, deep down, I wanted to have a family. A big family where we all love and accept each other. Something I thought we had when my darling wife was alive." Now Foster looked even more miserable. "But the moment she died, my sons ghosted me. They didn't want anything to do with me, and it took me a very long time to realize that it was my fault and not theirs for being stubborn."

"I can understand why you wanted what you had before," Thomas said quietly. "You were putting unrealistic expectations on them, and that's why they pushed back. They loved their mother and got away as soon as she was buried because you were too controlling."

Foster nodded. He sniffed and rubbed at his eyes. Was he actually close to crying?

"I thought finding them wives would make them grateful to me and then we would be able to talk. But it didn't work. I have a granddaughter, and I haven't seen her since the funeral." He swallowed. "I love Linda, and every time I hear how happy she is and what a joy she is with everyone, I feel sad. I can't be there for her, and I want to be. But Matthew... he refuses to speak to me."

Thomas could see the facade falling apart. Foster wasn't, deep down, a vindictive person as people believed. He was just scared, scared of being alone. So he lashed out in the wrong way so no one saw him as weak. It was human nature for a man to be strong, but Foster let it manifest in the wrong way. He had broken a lot of relationships with his actions, but there was still a bit of the real Arnold Foster in there. And he wanted out.

"I went about trying to get my sons back in the wrong way, but my stubbornness and my thought that I was the one in the right said it was the only way to get them back in line. My wife would tell me often that they are not soldiers or animals, but our children. Adults. I should let them be themselves and if I respect what they do, then I will have their respect and love in return. I forgot all that when she died. All of it." Foster rubbed his eyes. "It wasn't until I saw my six children marry people they're genuinely happy with that I remembered it. And what a fool I've been."

Thomas wasn't going to comment on that. But this was the most Foster had spoken to him, and the most he had seen the man so exposed emotionally. He was letting his guard down.

"You do come across as very abrasive, Mayor. A man not to be crossed. We're all wary of you."

"I wanted to be in charge. To be seen as successful,"

Foster grunted. "I got one part right, but the success? It doesn't make me happy. Neither does being in charge now. It feels hollow. I want the relationship I had with my children back. Or something close to it."

Thomas could understand that. And even though the Foster brothers showed hostility towards their father, he knew that there was a small part of each of them that wanted a relationship with their remaining parent. No one was going to give any time soon unless someone gave them a bit of a shove.

Thomas understood more than Foster realized.

"You can't force a relationship on them, Mayor. But you can start rebuilding it. I can't answer for all of them, but I do know if you start with a sincere apology to them and express what you wish for everyone, then they can make a decision on that." Thomas spread his hands as Foster brightened a little. "Maybe they'll forgive you and want to talk, maybe they won't. I can't answer for them, as I said. But you don't know until you try."

"I see." Foster thought for a moment. "That's my only option right now, isn't it?"

"Pretty much."

Foster thought for a moment. It looked like he was getting through to the man. Then Foster looked over Thomas's shoulder towards the house.

"I thought you would be off on your honeymoon by now."

"We're going later this afternoon. A few days isn't going to hurt while Pastor Michael gets things sorted."

"I see." Foster looked up at him and he smiled. Really smiled. "You're not too bad as a matchmaker, Pastor. You certainly pulled off something I wasn't expecting. I would've picked out really bad choices had I been left alone to it all."

Thomas now felt odd. He wasn't sure about a compliment from the man who had threatened his job. He chose his words carefully.

"You can do anything if you put your mind to it. You've said that yourself. It's going to take time, but it'll happen. Don't push things, or it'll never be what you want."

"As I've noticed." Foster held out a hand. "Thank

you, Pastor Thomas. I'll keep what you've said in mind."

It took a moment, but Thomas took the man's hand. His grip was still strong, but the man before him was completely different. It was a very surreal few seconds before Foster walked away, not as low as he had been before, but certainly in a different mood. Thomas was still trying to get his head around it.

"Thomas?" Tracy had come out of the house, heading down the path towards him. "What did Mayor Foster want?"

"He wanted to apologize."

"Are you serious?"

Thomas nodded.

"His sons shouted at him, and seeing his sons get married had him thinking. I think he's finally realizing that he doesn't always get his own way."

Tracy looked skeptical.

"Do you think he can be a decent person?" she asked.

Thomas wasn't sure, but he had seen a flicker of

what might have been the real man. He could see that coming out if someone kept him in line.

"Deep down he can. It's just going to take time to come out."

Tracy smiled and shook her head.

"You've got far too much faith in human nature, Thomas." She leaned over the gate, tugging his head down. "That's why I love you."

Thomas wasn't going to argue with his wife on that. So he kissed her and held her close. "Now, my love, let me take you away for a few days. Let's forget everything except love."

This was the final book in this much loved series. All the books can be read alone but if you would like to read them all, or you missed any, you can find them here

The day was so warm and bright that Jess Turner could hardly believe she was staring down into the newly dug grave. A light breeze made the thinner branches of the trees surrounding them sway. Their fresh green leaves rustled in the air and shimmered a little in the sun's bright rays. It was such a beautiful scene.

Meggie clung to her, a little drowsy and upset, although she was too young to know why. It was the only thing that made Jess truly sad; the idea that her three-year-old daughter would grow up without a father.

"Are you coping?" Katie Ellis whispered into her ear, her hand reassuringly on Jess's back.

"Yes," Jess mouthed silently when she turned to look into her best friend's eyes.

The service went on for what seemed like forever, although Jess heard barely a word of it. She had stopped listening from the very first. Unable to stomach the new young reverend describe Bart Turner, her husband, in such glowing terms. A father he might have been, but a good one? No. And as for being a good husband, surely Reverend Fisher was talking of another man altogether. Did the scant attendance at his funeral not tell him that Jess Turner's husband had never been a popular man? That his lack of popularity was linked so inextricably to his behavior towards others?

Meggie wriggled in her arms, her little head resting on Jess's shoulder. She was drifting into sleep and Jess knew it was for the best. Let her baby girl have no memory of this day. If Jess had anybody in the world to leave her daughter with, she would have, but the last of her family was being buried that day, and life as she knew it was never going to be the same again.

When the service was done, Katie Ellis took the

soundly sleeping child from Jess's arms. Meggie didn't wake, nor even stir, and Jess wondered what it would be like to be a child again; to have the sort of sleep that was blissful and uncorrupted by the day to day grind of life.

"Do you want a few moments alone, honey?" Katie asked in a whisper when the few mourners, most of whom were there out of pure curiosity, began to drift away.

There was to be no celebration of Bart's life; there would hardly be a person in all of Mallow Plains who thought there was anything there to celebrate. Not only that, but Jess could never have afforded to lay out the money for enough food to invite anybody back to her humble home, and everybody knew it. It was the only thing that felt all right about them being so poor. She didn't want to stand with the townsfolk who had become all but strangers to her over the years and discuss the life of a husband she would never truly mourn.

"What would I say?" Jess said and shrugged. "I can't think of a single thing to send him on his journey to the next world with." She paused for a moment, lowering her voice further still. "What sort of woman does that make me, Katie? What sort of woman cannot even say goodbye to her own husband?"

"One who has nothing to thank him for," Katie began, rising to her dear friend's defense by instinct. "One who was bullied and treated without heart of any kind, and that's the truth. You can't say what isn't in your heart, not for the new reverend, not for anybody."

"You always stand up for me," Jess said and smiled sadly. "No matter what."

"As you have always stood up for me. Husbands are one thing, honey, but best friends are quite another. Come on, let's go back to the house and fix something to eat. Meggie will be waking soon and grumbling if there isn't a little bread and butter for her." Katie smiled and the pair set off.

They walked the mile on foot, for Jess had no wagon, nor even a horse of her own. She was used to it, that was how things had always been for her, but she couldn't help but wish that life would let up once in a great while and send her just a little of its bounty.

They didn't talk much along the way, for Jess's tiny

house was partway up a steep hill and they were forced to exchange the adorable cargo that was Meggie more than once as they went. By the time they reached the house, both Jess and Katie were breathing hard.

Jess settled Meggie down on the battered little couch that was already in the house when she and Bart had first moved in. The landlord had behaved as if he had bestowed some great wedding present upon them. He had waved an arm flamboyantly over the piece of furniture which had already seen too much service by the time the Turners had moved in five years before.

"This house never felt like home to me," Jess said out of the blue as Katie set some water on the stove and cut what was left of the bread into thin slices.

"I know," Katie gently replied.

"But then Bart never felt like my husband. I was so horrified the day I was married to him and he brought me here. Not because of how impoverished it was; goodness knows the home I was raised in was no better."

"Because you never loved Bart and you knew you

never would. Home only feels like home when the people you love are there."

"That's true, Katie. It wasn't until Meggie arrived that I began to let go of the awfulness. Having a daughter didn't make me love Bart any better, it just gave me someone of my own to love until my heart didn't have room for anything more."

"She's a wonderful little girl." Katie left the stove and crossed the room to where Jess knelt by the couch.

"A wonderful little girl without a daddy," Jess said and felt guilt sweep over her.

When Bud Wallace had run to her just days ago with the news that her husband had been killed in a farming accident, Jess had felt nothing. She'd been numb, and that numbness had only been broken now and again with fear for how she and Meggie would manage. They had nothing now; how would they cope... would they lose even their home and having nothing? Bart had not been a good man and he tended to drink most of what he'd earned, but she had a roof over her head. Now what would she do?

"Do you know, I can't figure out which part of all this is making me feel so guilty? Is it, not feeling a thing for my dead husband, or the idea that I don't know how I'm going to spare my daughter the horror of the landlord throwing us out of here when I can't pay the rent?"

"It's not a day for guilt. No day is, honey. And you, of all people, have nothing to feel guilty for. There are folks who should feel guilty for the way they treated you in this life, but they're all gone now. It's the future you need to look to, not the past. That guilt won't serve you well and it isn't yours to hold, so let it go and concentrate on the world you've got now." Katie held out her hand, helping Jess to her feet. "So, let's have some tea and talk about the future. You're not alone, honey. You still have me."

And finally, for the first time since this nightmare began, Jess cried.

Grab this fabulous value box set for FREE with Kindle Unlimited here

To receive two free Mail Order Bride Romance join Fair Havens Books exclusive newsletter.
http://eepurl.com/bHou5D

If you liked this book you would love:

ON SALE 42 Book Box Set – Christmas Brides and Sweet Kisses FREE with KU

If you would like to find all of my books, look on my Amazon page

While there, click the yellow follow button for updates.

God bless,

Indiana Wake

The **Seven Lies**

Your Brain Is Telling You

**How Women Entrepreneurs Can Learn to
Lead Bigger, Charge More, and
Stop Shrinking**

MOLLY GIMMEL

The Seven Lies Your Brain is Telling You: How Women Entrepreneurs Can Learn to Lead Bigger, Charge More, and Stop Shrinking

Published by Vellamo Press

ISBN: 979-8-9946515-0-6

Paperback edition

Printed in the United States of America